"Peace is the result of retraining our mind to process life as it is, rather than as you think it should be."
—Wayne W. Dyer

Welcome to your world of peace and possibilities.

Welcome to living a life on purpose.

What people are saying about **Kim Ashton** and **A Guide to Living on Purpose**

Management of people and resources requires the ability to diffuse conflict at many levels. In high-pressure situations working in public relations and event management, I have utilized the very steps taught in Kim's book and her powerful leadership training. I found profound resolve and success. Thank you, Kim Ashton!

—*Melynda Thorpe Burt*, creative director/executive producer

Since working with Kim, I feel like I have become one-hundred-percent more effective and productive. As a wife, a mother of four boys and the CEO of my company, she taught me to see things for what they are. My biggest lessons revolved around setting boundaries, including how to say no; learning how to ask the right questions to get to the heart of a problem; and finding the courage to have difficult conversations. Kim has a gift for helping others discover answers and solutions on their own. She provided the tools and then allowed me to discover my own path.

—*Annelise Brown*, CEO and founder of Mialisia

I would highly recommend *A Guide to Living on Purpose*. Kim Ashton is gifted at taking complicated life concepts and explaining them in understandable, real-world terms. If you have a teen, I recommend this book as a springboard into adulthood. This book is an amazing gift to anyone who is looking to elevate their relationships and achieve the results they desire.

—*Michael Christensen*, entrepreneur, CEO, husband and father

Before meeting Kim, I lived life accomplishing and exceeding expectations; driving others to do the same. In my need for others to be just like me, I lost trust and respect amongst my staff, my friends and my family. Kim opened my eyes to another world. A world that infused leadership with trust and respect, ultimately increasing results. I learned how to accept myself while still evolving into an effective leader and taking control of my life. If you are looking to evolve yourself, continue to remain innovative, and become the leader of your life, make the choice to purchase Kim's book today. You will be so very grateful for that choice.

—*Lynn Mille*, human resource director

A Guide to Living on Purpose

Kim Ashton

Published by Open to the Possibilities
Copyright© 2016 Kim Ashton

ISBN 978-0-9972896-0-2

www.opentothepossibilities.live

Cover design and formatting by BookCoverCafe.com

In Gratitude

I know how those standing with an Oscar in their hand feel as they try to thank all of those that made their success possible. From my biggest cheerleader to my nemesis, you all made a difference and I heard what you said.

To my children: Luke, Katrina, Nicole, Ace, LaRa, Lindsey, Justin, Danielle, Todd, Devin and Chelsey, you are the loves of my life and the beat of my heart.

To my grandchildren: I hope I make you as proud of me as I am of you. This book is my gift and legacy to you. Pass it on and pay it forward.

Erika Merrill: you provided the feedback of a beloved mentor and trusted friend, even when I did not want to hear it. You are the sister I choose. Thank you for reading every page and ignoring the run-on sentences and horrible grammar. You saw past it all and into the heart of the message and the messenger.

Cousin Pat: an answer to a prayer.

All of my mentors who loved, pushed and supported: you called me out when I was playing small and cheered me on when I was playing big. You know who you are.

Annie: my pole driven deep into the ground that I can lean against when the storm is threatening to engulf me.

And to all of you who are willing to read this book, and do the work required to become the person you were meant to be.

Contents

When we set boundaries based on our values, we create trusting relationships with self and others.

Forgiving ourselves is about holding ourselves in a space of kindness, compassion, and love.

That which is not acted upon is not learned.

Foreword

Have you ever asked yourself, "Why didn't life come with an instruction guide?" and "What are the possibilities, both personally and professionally, if I knew how to live my life differently?"

In writing this interactive book, Kim has provided a catalyst for possibilities: possibilities that open the doorway for *impossible* to turn into *I'm-possible*.

I have known Kim for years. She has been one of the most influential women in my life. She is a mentor, facilitator, and coach, as well as a great friend, not only to me but so many. Kim is reliable, trustworthy, courageous, empowering, inspiring and much more. She draws from her own life experiences, creating both compassion and results while working with others.

When Kim asked me to read and give feedback on her book, I was a bit hesitant. I am not a big reader. After the first pages she sent me, I couldn't wait to receive more. Kim has a way of taking complex concepts and simplifying them in such a way that I knew I could easily integrate them into my daily life. I felt as if she was writing this book specifically for me. With each turn of the page, I was hungry to read on. Her real-life approach in this interactive book allowed me to make changes in my life. After reading and implementing the suggestions in Kim's book, I now have additional tools to make the best decisions for my life's direction and myself.

I love her unique concept of sections, knowing I could focus on what I wanted to work on versus reading it from beginning to end. This book allows us to read and identify what we need to stop doing (things that are not working), what we should continue to do (things that are working), and what to start doing that will get us what we desire in life.

Throughout the book, Kim asks provocative questions that focus on exploring and finding the best outcome for what we desire. Questions that allow an intricate look into creating balance in all aspects of our lives. There are also relatable stories and details on how to put your learning into action.

Quoting Kim: "What I know for sure is, in order for our personal and professional lives to have more success, freedom, and peace, we must be willing to be authentic and embrace change." At times change is not always a joyful journey; however, change is necessary to grow.

I got tremendous value out of reading this book. It gave me a new perception on how to work with others and myself. As a facilitator for youth and teens, I have been able to take what I have learned in this book and teach others. *A Guide to Living on Purpose* has a gentle yet powerful way of identifying what you want in life and making changes toward achieving those goals. Ultimately, having the life we were meant to have, rather than the one we dream about having.

Whether you read a little or a lot, this book is meant for you. So take action: purchase, read, relate, and begin living your life on purpose.

Erika Merrill
Customer service director
Facilitator

A Guide to Living on Purpose

I am writing this book as if you and I were curled up on your couch sharing, engaging, exploring, laughing, and crying like old friends.

When we purchase a new, much-desired product, we are often given an instruction guide. The purpose of this guide is to maximize the user's experience. Typically, we will skim through the guide, looking for sections that resonate with our need to know or to learn something. We peruse and index; we flip to the pages that promise to hold our answers. We read, we learn, and then we do what the instructions tell us to do.

When we become familiar with the way something works, we feel a sense of accomplishment in learning something new. In fact, we feel so good we know we could do it again. When we are ready, or in need of increasing our knowledge, we repeat the process and learn something new once again. In this way, we continue to build our knowledge and effective use of the product.

This book is an instruction guide to assist you in fulfilling the needs of your life. Needs such as:

- Improving your relationships
- Increasing your self-confidence
- Succeeding in your professional as well as personal life
- Challenging and letting go of old beliefs that no longer serve you

- Increasing the achievability of your goals
- Making the leap from where you are to where you want to be
- Giving yourself permission to stand in ownership of your life
- Switching your emotions quickly from reaction to response
- Finding courage and faith in the simple fact that you are enough, regardless
- Clearly defining your values; the guiding principles in your life
- Creating freedom, peace and success, both personally and professionally

As we are getting to know each other, my purpose in writing this book is to interrupt you. Interrupting ourselves begins with asking questions and then waiting for the answer. Sometimes we do not know the questions to ask, so we seek help with the mysteries we cannot see about ourselves.

I have provided some digging-deep questions at the end of each section that allow you to reveal yourself to you; the *real* you, not the one that your ego and image shows the world but the you that is spontaneous, joyful, wise, worthy, creative, forgiving, compassionate and trusting.

Trust that you are enough: enough to handle whatever is placed in front of you.

Trust that you are making the right choice for *you*, in the moment.

Trust the you that knows you are worthy of love, and the you who knows you make a difference.

Most people desire deep, authentic relationships. Deep, authentic relationships occur when we are willing to let go of judging ourselves. When we let go of judging ourselves, it is one million times easier to let go of judging others. Deep, authentic relationships with others will occur when we have one with ourselves. This guide is part of the journey in developing an authentic relationship with self.

As a young girl, I was given a ton of permission to be myself. My childhood was a happy one. I had friends and was loved by my parents. Lucky you, some of you are thinking.

As I moved into the early years of adolescence, I was filled with stirrings of desire; sexual desire was ever present. I tell my friends (and you and I are friends) that I did not smoke, drink or take drugs, but get me in the back seat of a car and it was a done deal. I'm not saying I was promiscuous; I am saying that sex was a heady mystery.

With most of life's mysteries, we all need someone to talk to, someone to guide us through the potholes, someone to give us advice so that when the time is right we can take life out for a spin ourselves. Unlocking the mysteries of living a life on purpose can be as titillating and confusing as the stirrings of sex.

Our lives and choices can be a heady mystery. Many years ago I owned a bookstore/café. I was so excited to become an entrepreneur. I found the perfect place, took out a loan, and did some remodeling. I installed a large chair with a reading lamp, and anyone who wanted to could curl up in it. The chair sat next to the window in an inviting corner away from the café area. The place was cozy and inviting. Smells of fresh coffee, homemade salsa and soups filled the air, and inviting music played.

I had customers of all kinds. There was a woman who would come a couple of times a month and sit in the large chair. I approached her when she first came, inquiring if she needed anything. She said "No" and left soon after. As she was leaving, I invited her to return any time.

I was surprised when she did return. She would walk in the door and head straight for the chair without saying a word. She didn't purchase anything or pull any books off the shelves. She would simply sit for about thirty minutes and then leave. This went on for months.

The bookstore was not a success. In my final week before closing, a man walked in. He sat at the counter and asked if I was the owner. I said that I was. He looked at me with tears brimming in his eyes and said, "You saved my wife's life. She's recovering from a childhood trauma. Unspeakable things happened to her. She would come in here and sit in your chair, and feel safe and at peace. I wanted to thank you and let you know that this place mattered."

I was $30,000 in debt and had saved a woman's life.

We never know when, where, how, or why we can meet the needs of others. Life and our journeys are indeed mysteries.

I recommend that you read the Worldview section first. Our worldview—how we perceive and interpret the world—is a foundational piece for change. In order to maximize our lives and live on purpose, change is required.

After reading the Worldview section, skim the titles of the other sections and determine which subject you want to focus on or become more proficient in, or which will help you identify the concept that has been evading you in living your life to the fullest. Read that section, practice the concepts, and infuse them into your life in such a way that they become automatic and conscious.

When you are ready, move onto the next evolution in your journey of living on purpose, select your section, and repeat the instructions above.

Practice sheets and journaling pages are provided. A brief overview follows the heading of each section so you can determine if the concept is one you are looking to implement. Each section stands alone; however, when used together the sections are woven into an amazing pattern to create freedom, peace and success, both personally and professionally.

Absolutely you can read this guide cover to cover. You have my permission to use it any way you desire. Remember, we are old friends.

Worldview

Our worldview is the lens through which we see the world. It is made up of all of the beliefs we have been taught and then adopted. Beliefs around what is good and bad, right and wrong, acceptable and not acceptable. Being willing to challenge those beliefs is the key to change and freedom.

Picture yourself as a small child. You are joyful, spontaneous, forgiving, innocent, honest, curious, trusting, intuitive, and creative. As life events unfold, you begin to develop and anchor yourself in those events, and call them your truth and reality.

I have an uncanny, deep-rooted belief that the world is a secure and safe place. My sweetheart calls it my "Pollyanna" outlook. This worldview can be attributed to my dad.

I grew up in a rural area in Utah called the Riverbottoms. Most families had over ten acres of land. We lived down the dirt lane from my grandparents.

We had horses and livestock. My parents and grandparents shared the responsibility, and milk, of one cow. My dad did the night milking, and I loved to walk with him up the lane to the barn to milk Bessy.

My dad was a construction worker. He stood six-two and was skinny as a rail. His hands are what I remember most, his large, calloused hands. Hands used to provide for his family; hands that were never raised in anger towards me.

It could be scary for a five-year-old to walk that dirt lane after milking, with only the stars and moon as light, and the symphony of chirping crickets and croaking frogs as noise.

One night, as my tiny hand was tucked inside my dad's rough one, his other hand gently swinging the pail of warm milk, he said, "Sweetheart, no need to be afraid." Then he did something surprising; he began to sing a catchy tune: "Whenever I feel afraid, I hold my head up high, and whistle a happy tune so no one will suspect I'm afraid."

I later learned this song is from *The King and I*. My dad always substituted some of his own words; the word is "erect" not "high," but my dad always said "high."

As I travel the highways and cities training leadership skills, there are times when I'm required to travel through the night due to weather and airplane groundings. I sleep in parking lots, truck stops, behind convenience stores, wherever I can, because I'm committed to being on time for my seminars in the morning. I have never once been afraid to do whatever it takes.

I'm not saying I'm reckless; no, I lock my car doors, bolt my hotel room door, and don't wander Central Park at night. I am saying that whenever I feel afraid, I hold my head up high, and whistle a happy tune so no one will suspect I'm afraid.

Thanks, Dad, for the worldview.

There are times when our worldview is not so happy; times when our worldview is molded by cruel, uncaring, angry hands and words. Words and actions that we take to heart, anchoring ourselves into thinking, believing and feeling that we don't matter, that we aren't safe, that we're not enough, and on and on. We go on owning and living out someone else's view of us.

In what way would your life be different if you challenged your worldview?

If we are lucky, as we grow our parents see it as their responsibility to instill in us some basic beliefs of what is good and bad, right and wrong, acceptable and not acceptable. They will have learned many of those basic beliefs from their own parents, and theirs and theirs, setting up and continuing generations of beliefs. Beliefs that work and beliefs that don't work.

Perhaps one of the lessons your parents wanted you to learn is to tell the truth. They reminded you that honesty is the best policy, and that if you tell the truth you won't get into trouble. One day you're sitting in the grocery cart at the checkout counter. As you're looking around curiously, you notice the person in line right behind you. In your honesty, you look that person in the eye and say, "You're fat."

Your parent immediately turns around and looks at the person. They know full well that you have made a truthful statement, but they are embarrassed at the social inappropriateness and tell you, in a firm tone, "Don't say things like that." They insist you apologize.

After you and your parent are out of earshot of the person you were honest about, your parent continues the dialogue about what is acceptable and not acceptable. Their tone and body language sends the clear message that you have done something wrong in being honest, in telling the truth. A belief is formed.

We spend our life attaching to, adopting, and agreeing with others' opinions and beliefs, and making them our own. This is normal, and is most often based on approval. Our childhood beliefs seem to have an iron grip on us. We are constantly seeking approval from our parents, childcare providers and teachers.

Merriam-Webster defines belief as "a state or habit of mind in which trust or confidence is placed in some person or thing." The problem is that our state or habit of mind in which we trust is based on what we have adopted. That trust or confidence that we have adopted may no longer apply or be relevant in our life. In fact, that belief may even be getting in the way of our living a peaceful, successful, life.

We were not born with a belief system based on religion, culture, political affiliation, west versus east, hierarchy of family, social status, or the definition of a good person. We were born into a belief system we usually adopt, and which has powerful, deeply embedded roots. Roots, we believe, that make us who we are. Our worldview has been repeated many times and reinforced with rewards and consequences.

Our worldview is learned, and anything learned can be unlearned.

Unlearning or testing a belief can be a lengthy process, and there are challenges along the way; challenges and costs that we may be unwilling to pay. There is constant pressure to conform. If we don't conform, our fear of being banished, cut off financially or physically, not included, or labeled are great motivators to not challenge our beliefs, our adopted worldview.

Generations of believing what is right and true, and what is wrong and bad can tip us to the side of war. Small personal wars with our neighbors and community can lead to global, life-altering devastating wars. Most wars on the home front and globally are fought over cultural differences or religion, all in the name of rightness based on beliefs and worldviews.

The devastation of rightness shows up in the following example.

The Hutu and the Tutsis of Rwanda are virtually identical. They share the same genes, the same language, and the same culture. About the only difference between the two groups is that the Belgians, who occupied Rwanda in 1916 made a decision to separate the two, like cattle, and favor the Tutsis. In 1994, the Hutus (who had been oppressed by the Belgians) took control of the government and methodically began exterminating the Tutsis. Over one million Tutsis were shot or hacked to pieces with machetes, all in the name of the addiction of rightness that had seized the Hutu people.

Most of us have not experienced the horror of this example. What we have experienced is the ways our worldview has created personal wars. How many times have we attached ourselves to something that our worldview dictates is good or bad, right or wrong, acceptable or not acceptable? We then go to war with a coworker, neighbor or family member. We retaliate with words and actions, attacking those we believe have treated us unfairly, unjustly, or wrongly.

By challenging our worldview, we begin to acknowledge how we get in the way. The ways that hold us back from changing and connecting. When we remember the profound words of Ronnie Dunn—"We all bleed red, we all taste rain, all fall down, lose our way, we all say words we regret, we all cry tears, we all bleed red"—we allow ourselves to soften, to see a commonality, and then, to possibly detach from our addiction to rightness.

When we're willing to detach from a misguided, often unfounded, rightness and challenge our worldview we find ways to create value with our coworkers, neighbors or family members. When we create value, we create influence. When we have influence, both parties will find ways to collaborate. When we collaborate, we are more successful.

We're very aware of the global wars that were and are being created in the name of religion/God. On a personal level, the fear of banishment and exile usually occurs when we push against beliefs, especially when we challenge the religious beliefs in which we were raised.

A dear friend of mine was caught up in a head-on collision of her truth and the teachings of the organized religion she was brought up with. She believed the basic, foundational teachings of the religion. She loved the sense of belonging she experienced, and she was well versed in the scriptures and doctrine. She had a pure knowledge of faith and God. She lived straddling the fence of her deepest desire to live her truth, which also belonged to a religion that demanded she be excommunicated for loving someone of the same gender.

She also knew that she was pushing up against the threads of society, but her fear was not of society; it was in losing something that she felt defined part of her: her religious belief. She was terrified of losing her immediate family, her anchor to God, her sense of belonging, and being shunned by her community. She confided in me that she felt she was living a lose-lose battle.

She was attending one of my workshops where we were practicing a strategic technique to help manage our emotions when conflict arises. I had each attendee partner with another attendee and sit facing each other. I invited them to bring to mind a conflict they were currently experiencing. I explained the first step in the technique: "Ask yourself what the situation is.'" In asking the question "What is the situation?" each person needed to take themselves and whomever they were in conflict with out of the equation.

In order to manage emotions and come to a resolution, it's not about the individual and it's not about the other person; it's about the situation.

Initially, the attendees struggled with the concept of removing themselves and the other person while getting feedback from their dyad partner. Most of them, however, began to grasp the concept as I walked around coaching and encouraging. My friend, however, was perplexed and stuck; she could not get past the idea that it was not about her or the church she belongs to.

I coached her, repeating, "No, that makes it about you. No, that makes it about them."

Just as I felt she was going to give up, her eyes went wide and she said, "The rules no longer apply!"

She had realized, in that moment, that she could have a relationship with God and give herself permission to do it a different way. The belief (rules) no longer applied. When she was willing to look at letting go of the belief she had adopted—that there is only one way to be in a relationship with God—she was free to explore other options that supported her.

Has it been an easy journey for my friend with regard to society and family? Not always. When people ask her what about her faith, she responds that it has taken courage, and even more faith, in a loving God to let go of beliefs that no longer work for her. What I know for sure is that she's finding ways to live a win-win life rather than a lose-lose one.

When we take the time to break conflict down to facts, our beliefs of good or bad, right or wrong, acceptable or not acceptable fall away, and we can move forward with a new perspective instead of a non-working attachment.

Guilt can, and most likely will, arise when we challenge our worldview. Guilt is a productive feeling. It's our signal, or flag, that our beliefs and actions are out of alignment.

Perhaps you have a belief that it's important to be helpful to your coworkers and a team player. With this belief you have become the company go-to person, the problem solver and solution finder.

You have worked diligently through the day to handle everything on your plate so you can leave on time at five P.M. You've made a commitment to be at your child's, niece's, nephew's (any person of value) ball game at five-thirty. It takes twenty minutes to get there, so you know you must leave at the stroke of five.

At four forty-five a coworker comes running in, hair on fire, requesting thirty minutes of your time. "I have to have my piece of a project completed by tomorrow at four P.M.," they tell you, "and I've run into a snag."

"I don't have thirty minutes," you say, and apologize profusely while your coworker stands there with disappointment clearly showing all over their face. With keys in hand, you finish up what you're doing and head out the door. As you walk to your car you're feeling guilty.

Your beliefs and actions are out of alignment.

Alternatively, you, being a team player, say, "Sure, I have thirty minutes." Keys in hand, you run to your car feeling guilty, rehearsing the apology to the person you broke your word to by being late.

Your beliefs and actions are out of alignment in both scenarios, hence the guilt.

What if your beliefs and actions could be aligned in a different scenario?

You, being a team player, tell your coworker, "I have ten minutes to give you, but I must leave right on five. I've made a previous commitment that I'm unwilling to break and can't reschedule. Will ten minutes help?"

"No, I need the full thirty," your coworker says.

You reinforce your message by saying, "I can't give you thirty minutes today, but I'm willing to come in thirty minutes early tomorrow. Will that work?"

"No, I don't want to do that. I like to exercise in the morning."

"Then I can't help you."

Have you been helpful? Yes. Have you been a team player? Yes. Your beliefs and actions are aligned.

Some of you may still feel guilty as you walk to the car. If that's the case it means you're attached, in some way, to the payoff you're getting by feeling guilty. This attachment to feeling guilty is likely based on your worldview, and it's in your power to change even that.

Please don't misunderstand me. I'm not giving you permission to run amok with the thought, "This doesn't work for me in this moment," and cast aside common sense. Nor am I asking you to let go of your beliefs on a whim.

I'm inviting you to challenge, examine, interrupt, and interview your worldview, especially in any areas where you were raised to view others that don't have the same worldview as you as bad, wrong, or unworthy of compassion and attention. I'm inviting you to see the world as a kaleidoscope of many changing colors, textures, and possibilities, in other words, to live on purpose.

In order for change to occur, you must be willing to challenge your worldview. I'm not suggesting you give up all of your beliefs; I *am* encouraging you to challenge them, to ask yourself, "Is this worldview that I have adopted still working for me in this moment?"

Being willing to challenge your worldview, and consciously choosing to do so are key to change and freedom. You will be giving yourself permission to live in the now and make moment-to-moment choices—choices free of past influences that hold you back from living a life on purpose, a life you design.

Journaling Page

I Am Listening to Me

Purpose

Purpose provides the anchor for all of our choices and actions. Knowing our purpose places us in the driver's seat of our lives. Once we are clear on our purpose, we can begin the journey of achievement by also including and implementing vision and goals.

Purpose provides the anchor for all our choices and actions. Knowing and anchoring to our purpose dramatically increases the likelihood of achieving what we desire. The other variables are intention, vision, goals, and method/how. This section will guide you step by step through each variable.

Have you ever been passionate about a new relationship, business venture, weight-loss plan or dream home? Often, it isn't long before the excitement turns to disappointment and failure is on the horizon. This failure leaves you feeling deflated and wondering what went wrong. *How could I have let myself down,* you ask yourself. *Why is it so hard for me to succeed?*

More often than not the reason your excitement turns to disappointment, with failure on the horizon, is because you were not anchored to your purpose. Everything starts with an intention; intention is the *want* in the formula.

What I want: a loving committed relationship; a business venture to increase my income by ten percent; a weight-loss plan that will work for me; a dream home where I can raise my children and decrease my footprint on the environment.

Next comes purpose. Purpose is the reason why you want your intention to come to fruition. It's part of the human condition to declare what we want and then jump straight to how we're going to get it. If we stop, slow down, and make sure we're clear about why we want it, the door of possibilities becomes wide open to achieving our intention.

As an independent contract trainer, I worked with a company that provided attendees with the opportunity to walk on fire at the completion of their training. I had never walked on fire, so I joined them one evening. Excitement and a bit of fear surged through my thoughts. When we arrived at the site of the event we formed a circle, and the facilitator guided us through a dialogue around what it might take to move past the belief—the personal knowledge—that fire burns. He informed us we would be part of the process of building and preparing the fire that evening. And it would be our choice whether to walk or not.

There was a spiritual aspect around the process of building the fire. The wood was cedar, and the aroma filled my senses as I carried a piece to be expertly placed to ensure even burning. The process of building the fire was done in silence, and I felt honored to participate.

As the bonfire was lit and the flames roared into the sky, the facilitator expertly instructed us on the power of purpose, the *why* we would be walking, and reminded us that we had a choice in walking or not that evening. He gave us permission to choose for ourselves.

When the fire had burned down to coals, we each had a turn at spreading them out with a rake. As I took my turn raking the coals into a fifteen-by-fifteen-foot rectangle, the heat singed my eyelashes and eyebrows. I had to turn my face away for fear of being burned. My internal dialogue screamed: *There's no way I'm taking off my shoes and doing this. No way.*

When the walkway was prepared to the facilitator's satisfaction, the rectangle of hot glowing coals was bordered with water-soaked strips of carpet. We were instructed to remove our shoes and socks, and reminded again that by no means did this constitute a commitment to walk. The facilitator simply wanted us to be ready.

We were handed an index card and asked to write down our purpose, the *why* we were walking. He repeated that walking was a choice and we could choose not to, especially if our purpose was not clear.

I remember scribbling something down, knowing I had no purpose, no anchor. My fear was driving me as I watched the hot glowing coals. Even as I watched person after person declare their purpose and take their first step, then the next and next, walking the length of the rectangle, arriving unscathed, I didn't believe or think myself "enough" to do it.

I took a deep breath and approached the top of the glowing coals, then backed away, unsure. My ego taunted me: *Just go. You don't want to be the only one that doesn't go. How embarrassing will that be?* I approached one more time and, while standing at the start, repeated in my mind: *Why?*

What is my purpose? Why? Then I heard a whisper: *Trust you.* The night became quiet as I anchored in those words.

I took my first step, knowing my purpose, my *why*. My anchor would carry me across the glowing coals that night and through a majority of my life. When the going gets tough, I remember those two whispered words: *Trust you.*

It's imperative that your purpose is grounded in clarity rather than ego. As I participated and co-facilitated many fire walks, I can assure you that those who ended up with burn blisters on the bottoms of their feet were the ones that were ego driven. I'm sure I would have ended up with blisters if I'd listened to my ego and walked.

When the ego sneaks in and tries to run the *why*, we may be deceived into believing that we have found our anchor. Be cautious; there is a huge difference between ego-driven purpose and clarity-driven purpose. Here are a few examples:

Intention: I want a loving relationship. Ego-driven *why*: so I don't have to be alone.

- Intention: I want a loving relationship. Clarity-driven *why*: to share my life with someone that is committed to respect, honesty, joy and abundance.
- Intention: a business venture that increases my income by ten percent. Ego-driven *why*: so I can prove to my family that I did amount to something.
- Intention: a business venture that increases my income by one hundred percent. Clarity-driven *why*: to provide financial independence, enjoy my life to the fullest, and share what I have.
- The ego-driven purpose is about proving something. Not only can we be deceived by an ego-driven purpose but we can also

make the mistake of grounding ourselves in what we don't want. When you set your foundation on what you don't want you literally build your intention on shifting sand, and it makes that intention almost impossible to achieve.

I was coaching a client, a very successful businessman whose second marriage of fifteen years was falling to pieces. He had worked diligently to make it succeed, so diligently that he had lost pieces of himself and no longer knew who he was. His business was suffering. His friends continued to ask him what was wrong, for those caring friends heard the pain and distraction in his voice.

We were at a pivotal point in our conversation; it was clear his intention was to save his marriage. I calmly and directly asked, "What is your purpose in saving your marriage?"

His immediate reply: "Because I don't like to fail."

I looked him straight in the eye and told him that was the wrong reason. His answer was based on what he did not want versus the clarity of knowing why he wanted to save his marriage.

I asked him again, "What is your purpose, not what you don't want but what you do want?"

A look of surprise showed up on my client's face as he realized he was anchored in not failing. As we continued to drill down, he reported that what he really wanted was a peaceful, loving relationship.

The minute your mind has the thought *I don't want*, ask yourself what you do want. Keep asking the questions: *Why do I want this? What is my purpose?* Continue to drill down until you know, and your *why* is clear. Remember, you're looking for your anchor, the foundation that keeps you grounded.

Many times you may think you're at your purpose when where you really are is at the surface of the *why*, not wanting to go deeper for fear you might not get what you want. It can feel like a bare-knuckle street fight with yourself.

Challenge yourself. Ask yourself: *Am I at the anchor that's going to drive my actions and choice? Is this the why I'm willing to lean up against when the going gets tough, as tough as feeling alone in the dead of night with failure howling at my door? Or is this my ego talking, hanging on for dear life with the desire to prove something? What is my purpose?*

Purpose provides the anchor for all of your choices and actions. Knowing your Purpose places you in the driver's seat of your life, and gives you an anchor to the choices and actions you take moving forward. Knowing the purpose/the *why* of your intention allows you to navigate through the tough times.

Simply remembering/anchoring in why you're doing what you're doing will give you an immediate sense of peace and realignment, opening up powerful possibilities that you didn't notice before.

Vision: What I see/who I see involved

This is the step involved with "seeing" your intention manifest. See yourself sharing your life with someone that is committed to joy and abundance, a life that gives you financial independence while you enjoy yourself, living life to the fullest, sharing what you have, having a healthy body and making wise choices as to what goes in it, hearing the laughter of friends and family while minimizing the effects of your life on the environment. See your purpose.

I am an advocate of vision boards. This is a visual representation of your dreams: where you want to be, and what you want to achieve. The purpose of a vision board is to be a daily visual reminder of who you want to become, where you want to live, what you want to change in your life, and what aspirations you have personally, professionally, physically, financially, relationally, emotionally, or all of the above.

When your board is complete, place it in a spot where you will see it every day. In the business world, a new trend is for companies to create department or team vision boards. What a great collaboration tool.

Supplies you will need to create a vision board:

- Poster board or matte-finish board of any size or color. Determine the size that is going to work best for your space.
- A variety of different magazines, the more options the better. You can obtain magazines from libraries, doctors' and dentists' offices, hair salons, family and neighbors. You can also print out pictures and sayings from your computer.
- Glue sticks
- Scissors

Before you begin, sit quietly for a moment. Close your eyes and envision what it is you desire and who might be involved. Feel the energy of accomplishment, the excitement of the journey. Now open your eyes and start leafing through the magazines, being inspired by what you see and read. Tear out the articles or pictures that interest you. Some of you neater ones might want to cut them out, but I personally like the tearing.

For instance, my sweetheart and I committed to live by a budget for one year (the intention). We wanted to create clarity and peace about where our money was being spent in order to focus on minimizing our debt and increasing our retirement funds (the purpose).

We went to a neutral place, a small, quiet room at our local library, to have the difficult and revealing conversation around money. After four hours, a lunch break, bathroom visits, and a few cooling-off breaks, the budget was complete. We agreed to take it one step further and create a visual manifestation of our commitment to being the stewards of our money by creating a financial vision board together.

The following Saturday we grabbed the piles of magazines I keep for the Women's Leadership Retreats I facilitate, glue sticks, scissors, and a half-sheet of poster board, and started tearing and cutting out pictures and words that would support us in bringing our intention to fruition. We gave ourselves twenty minutes; a timeframe is a great idea because it will allow you to choose between inspiration and deliberation.

Deliberation or sorting through can occur when you're gluing items to your board. As we laughed and shared what this saying meant or this picture meant, the board took on a life of its own; a life that we could both align with. Finally the board was complete and we both had small piles of discarded pictures and sayings.

With a sly grin, my sweetie pulled out a picture of a beautiful new car. "I know this is a dream, and we certainly don't have the finances for this now, or even in the near future, but I so want it."

I laughed and said, "Honey, this is a dream board: let's glue it to the back."

We taped the vision board to the French doors in our bedroom that lead onto the deck, giving us not only a visual of the front but ensuring that we saw the item glued to the back every day.

Not only was that a peaceful year—a year of discipline, diligence and diversification—but at the end of it there was a beautiful, black, gently used Ford Fusion (we call it the Bat-mobile) sitting in the driveway.

See it. Dream it. Create it.

Goals: Steps/when

Statistically most people achieve 33 percent of the goals they set in their lifetime: 33 percent. No wonder most of us let out a groan when we hear the word "goal" and think, *Thanks for another opportunity to fail. Yippee.* As a performance coach, I found this number to be staggering and true at the same time.

We have many tools available to set and achieve goals, the most common of which is SMART: Specific, Measurable, Attainable, Realistic and Timely. What, then, is the problem? Why the staggering rate of unachievable goals?

Then it dawned on me. When do we ever talk about obstacles that get in the way of achieving the goals we set both personally and professionally? Maybe the problem is not with the tools we use to set the goal, but in not being *aligned* with the goal due to our mindset.

When we set a goal there is a mindset, because realistically anything is attainable. The question that creeps in this: *What am I going to have to give up to attain it?* We become focused on this question instead of having an authentic conversation with ourselves, our bosses, or our team about the obstacles that could get in the way of achieving our goal.

It doesn't stop with stating what the obstacle may be. You also need to have a conversation about solutions for getting through the obstacles so you can achieve the goal.

This part of the formula is focused on the steps you need to take to achieve your intention:

- Intention: to purchase a house.
- Purpose: to provide a nurturing space for myself, spouse, children and others to grow, create, laugh, be themselves, and feel safe in an environment of possibilities.
- Vision: Five bedrooms, three baths, large master-bedroom closet, enough space for a garden, secluded neighborhood, supportive school.
- Goal: to set a budget amount. Spend three hours on Saturdays looking through model homes and neighborhoods, and check out the location at different times of the day. Ask friends to recommend the most affordable closing company. Break down the steps into finite pieces, each of which will require a timeframe and action.

How: Mechanics to achieve intention

You live in California and your *intention* is to travel to New York. Your *purpose* is to connect with family and friends. There are numerous ways to get to New York, including walking, going by bike, car, skateboard or train, hitchhiking, flying, and so on.

The *how* I am speaking about is this: you are focused on the best, fastest and cheapest way to travel to New York, so you choose to fly.

You have done your homework and worked it all out. In Minneapolis there's a thunderstorm and you miss your connection. The *how* of being the best, fastest, cheapest just went out the window.

There are a multitude of ways to get to New York; if you do whatever it takes, that is a powerful place to be standing when the *how* falls through. If you start out on a plane to New York and the plane is grounded, instead of giving up, rent a car. If the rental car gets a flat and you don't know how to change it, find someone who does.

By staying anchored in your purpose, the windows of possibilities will be wide open. Find a way. Plus, you have just added having an adventure to your intention.

Intention. Purpose. Vision. Goal. How. This is a simple and effective formula to achieving your desires and feeling fulfilled, accomplished, and successful.

If there comes a time when, for whatever reason, you don't get your desired outcome, be kind with yourself. Retrace your journey, notice where you got off course, and learn for next time. Don't abandon the formula; it works. Remind yourself that you're new at this, and that excellence in any area requires practice and patience.

When you do reach your desired outcome, celebrate.

Practice Page

Bring to mind what's next for you. What is your desire? What do you want to be different?

Intention (want):

____

____

____

Purpose (why):

____

____

____

Drill down; get to the bottom line.

____

____

____

Vision (who and what do you see):

____

____

____

____

Goals (what, steps to be taken):

____

____

____

____

- Obstacles getting in the way of you achieving your intention:

____

____

____

- Solutions to the problems, and possible ways of getting through any obstacles so you can achieve your intention:

____

____

____

How (mechanics to achieve the goal):

Journaling Page

Honoring Me and My Destiny

Accountability/ Ownership

There is a significant difference between being accountable for the choices we make and seeing ourselves as victims of those choices. By examining the difference between accountability and blame, we begin to see the value of ownership versus the fear of getting into trouble.

Personal accountability means accounting for our choices; knowing that we had a part in the outcome and owning it, whether the outcome worked or did not work. For most people, this accountability conversation is a hard pill to swallow; it certainly was for me. I had many a tearful conversation with my performance coach as I tried to wrap my head around the concept of owning my part in an outcome, especially when it failed.

When we're younger and something gets damaged or broken, our parents might say, "Who's accountable for this?" What they're really asking is who is going to be punished, spanked, grounded, or lose their allowance. Most of us learn early on to quickly say, "Not me." And then we fill in the blank with someone else's name, usually a sibling, the family pet or the neighbor kid, because who really wants to be in trouble?

We continue the not-me attitude into adulthood. This leads to finger pointing and the someone-else-is-to-blame mentality. Lack of accountability is defined as being a victim: being a victim of others, a victim of circumstances, with accompanying excuses, justification, and blame. Being a victim is commonplace in society, and in some cases has a huge payoff, many times financial.

To be very clear, there is a distinct difference between being a victim and being victimized.

Many people spend years perfecting ways of being the victim of someone else. The victim mentality consists of taking an intricate and often elaborate set of steps. The minute anyone takes any of these steps, they are firmly planted in victim mentality. The steps may look like, but not be limited to:

- Minimize the broken agreement; it's not a big deal, nobody cares. *I know I said I would be to the meeting on time, but most people show up late so who cares?*
- Justify the behavior: create an excuse or story around why it happened. *Bill held me up. You know what a talker he can be, and I just couldn't get away.*
- Make someone else wrong: use words like she's not, he's not or they're not. *Well, Jill didn't complete her portion of the project until the eleventh hour, so what could I do about it?*

- Avoidance: unwillingness to be uncomfortable in owning up. *He borrowed a book and never returned it, so now I don't have to take his phone calls and can avoid him at the grocery store.*
- Get agreement: create a "posse" to reinforce how wrong they are so you can feel better about you. *I never want to be on a project with Joe again because he's such a slacker. Don't you agree?*
- Perceive negatives: "all men" or "all women," worst-case thinking. *All corporate executives have forgotten what it was like to be one of the little guys.*

We go to great lengths to avoid handling broken agreements, and expend energy in not being accountable or being a victim. We ask ourselves if there's a simpler way—a way to accept that we are accountable for our part in the outcome.

There is, and that simpler way is explained in this section. The simpler way is to use an inquisitive step-by-step technique to stop the madness of assigning blame, and justifying our actions. We need to dramatically change the conversation from not being in charge of our lives, from claiming that we are simply blown this way and that by the whims of circumstances and the actions of others to claiming ownership of our lives, and empowering ourselves and those around us to be accountable and move forward.

In order to change our mindset, we must let go of the belief that accountability has anything to do with someone else being at fault, wanting someone else to be in trouble.

We run the stories: I did my part on the project; I gave a hundred percent to the marriage; I met the expectations and so-and-so did not. "Why am I being punished?" we ask in our whiney voice. Those with a victim mentality do this constantly, time and time again. I'm not saying there are no consequences when the outcome doesn't meet the desired results. I'm saying that to be accountable, we must shift our focus from blaming others to accepting our part in event. And looking at what I can learn from the outcome that will allow me to move forward.

What if there was no blame? What if there was simply a gentle conversation about what our part was in the outcome, and we took ourselves on a journey, a learning process? What a great idea. But wait. No, I wasn't the one who screwed up/cheated/was unclear/didn't meet expectations ... and once again we're off and running, falling back on blame and justification.

Being accountable takes discipline, and the ability to put our ego aside for a moment to create ownership versus being a victim of our circumstances.

I have an issue with people who are late. In fact, it is one of my hot buttons. I am obsessive about being on time, at times annoyingly so. I have been given feedback about how aggravating my showing up half an hour early can be. I'm very methodical about time, calculating how much time it will take me to get to where I need to be. I factor in traffic and possible accidents. Wow, writing this makes me realize that I sound a bit on the creepy side.

I had an important meeting that was going to take forty-five minutes to get to if traffic flowed well. I knew that in order to be on the safe side I needed to give myself an hour and fifteen minutes. Yes, I am methodical.

Things were going smoothly as I was getting ready, and I was managing time effectively until a conflict arose that needed my full attention, eating away at my best-laid plans. Keys in hand, I was out the door at the forty-five-minute mark. Reaction, stress, discomfort, justification; I was already preparing my apology speech, running full throttle through the justification list.

The road out of my neighborhood is posted at twenty-five miles an hour, and not only was my mind running at full throttle but my foot on the gas pedal was also. Yep, red-and-blue flashing lights behind me two minutes after I pulled out of my driveway, sealing the fate of my worst nightmare—being late. As the officer approached my car, I had my insurance card and driver's license in hand. I didn't even try pleading my case; I was going fifteen miles over the speed limit. I believe that could be considered a criminal offense.

As the officer was walking back to his vehicle to check if I was a convicted felon, I was working very hard at calming myself down, interrupting and intervening the fault, blame and justification talk running through my head. I decided to spend my energy and focus in a much more productive manner by being accountable. I asked myself: *What do I get to learn in this moment? What's the lesson that's unfolding for me?*

There seemed to be a pause in the universe while I ran a technique that not only allows for ownership but also brings a what's-next and what-am-I-learning component. Accountability formula:

- I am accountable: For being late. (It's my fault if I'm late speaks to blame)
- What is my belief? Being on time shows respect; being late shows disrespect.
- What is my attitude? Only lazy, unconscious people are late.
- What is my assumption? Being on time or early makes me better than others (oh my gosh, this was the most revealing part for me).

- How does this show up in my life; is it a pattern? There are places in my life where I'm very judgmental of others. I often see myself as better than them (a double wow and a dose of holy crap).
- My new choice is to let go of my attachment to perfection in myself and others, and to have authentic conversations rather than I-am-right, you-are-wrong conversations.

In that moment I knew that getting a speeding ticket was a gift I had given myself. The naked revealing of my arrogance took my breath away, and was a much needed wake-up call.

As the officer approached my car the second time, I was crying joyfully (I suspect he didn't think they were tears of joy) and open-heartedly thanked him for the ticket and the time to learn a valuable lesson (the look of surprise on his face was priceless). When he handed me the ticket, he stated that he wrote it for nine miles over, and he appreciated me being cooperative.

Most of us have a tendency to jump straight from "I am accountable for being late" to "My new choice is to be on time." No, no, no. There's so much going on in between the leap from late to on time that requires discovery. When we bypass the juicy middle—the belief, attitude, assumption, and how this shows up in our lives—we miss a learning that is valuable. We bypass the value in the new choice.

It takes less time and energy to run the accountability formula than to minimize, justify, make someone else wrong, avoid them, get agreement, perceive negatives and then do it again.

We are human. We are going to make mistakes. The definition of a mistake/failure should be: *I saw the opportunity to learn and I took it.*

Our mistakes and our failures are placed in our path to learn from. Are you taking the time to learn from mistakes and failures, and letting go of the tired old game of being a victim?

Accountability means being responsible for and desiring to account for our choices. By owning our choices we shed the bondage of fault, blame and regret. It's time to tip the scale from fault, blame and justification to ownership.

It's time to own up. Owning up equals powering up. By owning up we create powerful relationships and lifelong lessons. By owning up we give permission for others to follow our lead in reframing accountability as ownership. By standing in our results we see the magnitude of how powerful we really are to shape and create the life we deeply desire.

Practice Page

I am accountable for

____

____

____

____

What is my:

• belief (what I bring to the party based on my history)

____

____

____

____

• attitude (position or posturing)

____

____

____

____

- assumption (what is or isn't true, and what I have made up that led to my choice)

How does this show up in my life? Is this a pattern?
(The juicy middle that provides the opportunity to reveal.)

My new choice is
(Don't be surprised if this has nothing to do with what you are accountable for.)

Journaling Page

Doing it Differently

Neutrality

When we are in a reactionary state it's almost impossible to think clearly. In this reactionary state we say and do things that are not in our best interest or the best interest of the desired outcome. Learning to respond after we react is a key element in self-discipline and emotional well being.

Many of us have lost our way when it comes to managing our emotions. Life is filled with pressure to exceed expectations, both personally and professionally. Most of us experience pressure, but the problem comes when we turn that pressure into stress. Pressure does not always have to equate to stress. Pressure is the urgency of something demanding our attention. We have pressure regarding clients, relationships, time, physical well being, career issues, traffic, health, and so on.

Stress is our internal reaction to pressure; bottom line, stress is self-induced. We feel pressure and automatically leap to being stressed instead of focusing on what we can control. What if the client isn't happy? Verses. How can I make the client happy? What if my relationship/marriage fails? Verses. What's it going to take to create a loving, peaceful, lasting relationship?

Most of our ancestors didn't throw their arms in the air and scream, "I'm all stressed out!" No, they rolled up their sleeves and built, created, got stuff done. And they had pressure; it was simply different than ours.

Is pressure bad for us? No. In fact, it can help strengthen our ability to cope. There is also productive pressure; pressure placed on a group or individual to make decisions factually and quickly. Pressure can also build our time-management and problem-solving skills.

The problem arises when we react internally to pressure. We climb on the what-if hamster wheel. We're simply going in circles, never getting anywhere.

Stress is taking a serious toll on our physical, emotional, relational, spiritual, and financial selves. We overeat, overdrink, overspend, overexercise, view excessive television, play too many video games, and share too much personal information on social media, all in the name of reducing our stress. High blood pressure is on the rise, lack of a good night's sleep is at epidemic levels, and losing control of our emotions happens way too often.

The reason we experience stress is simple: we worry. We worry about whether the client will be happy, if our spouse will be faithful, if we will arrive on time, if our children will grow up to be contributing adults, if the company will make money this year, if, if, if, if.

The definition of worry is paying interest on a loan you have not yet received. If you *would* be willing to pay interest on a loan you don't yet have, I highly recommend Dave Ramsey's Financial Peace course. Paying interest does not pay down principle. We have to stop the spin of if, if, if and focus on what it's going to take, and what we control.

What if we could begin to manage our emotions and find our neutrality? In order for that to happen we need to examine the basic difference between reaction and response. We also need to ask ourselves what our part was in the outcome.

Many of you have seen the formula $E + R = O$ (event + reaction = outcome). We're going to break it down and look at it in a different way, a way that can be a tool for finding neutrality.

Events occur in our lives on an hourly or daily basis. The ones we react to are usually the ones that begin with this premise: *this should/ should not be happening.*

We react; this is normal. It's part of our fight-or-flight response. Our brain is trying to make sense of something unexpected or that we believe is dangerous. The biggest problem is that we take action based on this fight-or-flight state.

I do know it's more complex than this, and I'm really working on making it simple so you will be willing to do something different.

We usually cannot control the event (E) portion of the equation; things happen even when we plan extensively. Life is often not in our control.

Our reaction (R) to the event is usually automatic. We're reacting to something unexpected; something we believe should or should not have occurred. In this reaction state, our fight-or-flight response usually kicks in. When we take action from a reactionary state, more often than not it's when the outcome is not what we desire.

I travel often for my work of facilitating and speaking. The job I would never want is the customer-service counter at the airport in the middle of a snowstorm; people have gone insane. While waiting in line I hear, "Call somebody." I want to respond with, "Who would you like them to call? God or Mother Nature?"

In situations like this people are often in such a reactionary state that they walk away screaming, "You'll be hearing from my attorney," without having waited for a solution to their dilemma. The outcome is they still have no way of getting to their destination; they are in a reactionary state and cannot think clearly. Reaction, fight or flight, is not a state of problem solving; it is a state of reacting.

I will often step up to the counter and say, in a calm tone, "I would like to find the quickest way to my destination and I need your help in doing so." The person behind the counter will look at me like an angel has just been delivered. By being in a calm, responsive state I have gotten the last first-class seat on a flight, food and hotel vouchers (if the flight is delayed due to weather they don't have to provide either), and a representative willing to accommodate and research a multitude of options to facilitate my desired intention—getting to my destination.

We react when an event occurs that is surprising. After reacting, we must not take action. What we need to learn to do is pause, pause, and pause. Pause until we are in a responsive (R) state. We may not be able to control the event; however, we can learn to condition ourselves to turn reaction into response. By pausing, we give ourselves time to gather our thoughts before we take action. This process of pausing takes discipline, but it's well worth the payoff because the outcome will be significantly different in a responsive state than a reactionary one.

It's also important to remember that we're not reacting to the snowstorm; we're reacting to the connecting flight we will miss, or the cruise we've spent the past three years saving for. Being in a responsive state (problem solving) will get us closer to our outcome than a reactive state (fight or flight).

Will you always get everything you want in a responsive state? No. What you will get, though, is more peace, freedom, success, and a healthier life.

When we are in a reactionary state, our perception, emotion and ego are also involved. Our perception is our reality, and our reality is no one else's. Our perception is based on our worldview, making it 99-percent irrational. The reason it's irrational is that our worldview is based on our past experiences, so we're trying to make sense of something surprising or unexpected from the past, rather than being present in the moment with this new experience.

This is why it's important to manage our emotions and be neutral; this allows us to slow down, pause, and see things as they are in this moment. Then we take action from a rational/responsive place versus a reactionary place.

Some statements that you can quickly ask yourself to help create a pause, interrupting your perception so you can get your head straight before taking action:

- What is really going on?
- What am I unwilling to notice? What am I avoiding?
- Is this my circus, and are these my monkeys?
- What am I making up?
- How bad is it really, compared to other parts of the world?
- What are the facts?
- How bad will this seem in ten weeks, ten months, ten years?
- Is this my path, my journey; are these my lessons?

Emotion is not a bad word. Let's pull the word apart: *e* is the symbol for energy, so emotion is energy in motion. This is why we cry, vent, yell, hit things; energy gets trapped in our bodies and we want it out.

Many businesses are adopting a two-minute venting rule. There will be various offices within the organization where an employee can go and for two minutes say anything, just let it out, and it will not be held against them. At the end of two minutes they're asked how they're going to handle the issue, or what will be their course of action moving forward.

This process takes no more than ten minutes to unfold, and moves people from reaction to response before they take action.

It is reported that, by having this safe outlet, negativity and gossip have decreased and productivity has increased, because people are not harboring ill feelings and being distracted by holding in pent-up emotions. It is also contributing to increased problem-solving skills.

There is a big difference between venting and complaining. Venting is focused on getting it out and moving forward to problem solving or the what's-next conversation. Complaining is simply telling the story over and over, with little or no interest in finding a solution or moving forward.

I recommend you find an accountability buddy that you can vent to (I like to call it throw up all over) for no more than two minutes. Then that person can ask, "How are you going to handle that?" or "What action are you going to take?" Too often we regurgitate a story over and over and over. Stop! Be healthy and forward moving, keeping your energy in motion.

We all have emotions. What most of us are not used to doing is identifying our *true* emotions. We move straight to anger, frustration or being pissed off, but these are secondary emotions. When we go straight to anger, frustration or being pissed off, we have bypassed the underlining emotion.

The five most common non-working emotions that show up in the workplace are when people feel disrespected, disappointed, embarrassed, jealous, or helpless. Feelings are not bad. Start identifying how you are feeling.

When we are in a reactionary state, we can almost be assured that our ego is involved in some way. Our ego is necessary; its job is to keep us safe. The problem is that we give our ego way too much permission, especially when we're reacting; ego = energy go!

When we're in a reaction state, our ego is usually attached to one of two thoughts: *I want to be right* or *I don't want to be wrong*. Which one applies to you? What are you attached to, the need to be right or the fear of being wrong? Some of you will be very clear about your answer, some of you will be stumped, and some of you will feel it's situational. That's all right.

I'm really clear about mine. I want to be right. You can make me wrong all day long and I'm not attached. But if I get anchored in being right, it's really hard for me to back off or down.

There are many attachments harbored in our unconsciousness that can cause us to take action immediately after we react, and our right-wrong conversation is a powerful one. By becoming familiar with our attachment to either being right or not wanting to be wrong, we have the conscious knowledge to pause before we take action. We have the knowledge to ask ourselves: *What am I attached to?*

A key component in being neutral and coming from a responsive state is the ownership of the statement: *Every outcome I have, I had a part in.* This concept sits sideways with most people.

Now wait a minute, you may be thinking, with a dose of healthy skepticism, that can't be right. How can I believe that every outcome I have, I had a part in? But what if you believed that you did *not* have a part in every one of your outcomes? That is the moment when you must gently begin pulling the thread, and unwind, explore, retrace your thoughts, and notice your actions.

When I made this statement in one of my seminars, a young woman's hand shot straight in the air. I called on her and she stated in a definitive voice: "I disagree. I work for the government in the welfare department, and I volunteered to take on the overflow of complaints for a month. One woman was screaming at me, saying that I denied her welfare and asking what I was going to do about feeding her kids. I did nothing to this woman. What part did I have in her being denied her welfare?"

One of the other attendees in the room raised her hand and I called on her. She asked if she could answer the question, and I told her to give it a shot.

"First, you work for the welfare department," she said to the young woman. "People see you as the government. And second, you volunteered to take the complaints."

A quizzical look appeared on the young woman's face, followed by a sense of calmness as she grappled with the simplicity of her part in it. "I get what you mean," she said, "but I still don't agree."

The room laughed wholeheartedly.

Sometimes we can't see how simple this concept is because our nose is pressed up against the glass of the picture. When we allow ourselves to take ten steps back, we see the bigger picture, bringing clarity to our part in it. This is why, at times, it's easier for others to see our part, but we want to hang onto our rightness about how wronged we were, negating any possibility of neutrality.

Again, the purpose of unraveling your part is not to decide right or wrong, or that life is fair. The purpose is to ask: *Where do I take action, moving forward, to a neutral place?*

You may be planning a cruise, and there is an option to purchase travel insurance. Something inside you whispers: "Purchase travel insurance." You ignore it, because you were worried (there is that word again) about the added expense or something else. Unwind it, and you then have power and choice.

This doesn't mean that you always have to purchase travel insurance. It may mean you will consider the insurance if you're taking a journey that has time-sensitive connections in the middle of winter and you're traveling through Denver. And I'm fairly confident that listening to the still, quiet voice has served many of you on numerous occasions.

It doesn't mean you will never volunteer for anything again. But it might mean that you prepare yourself for the inevitable, conflicting conversations, and have the neutrality to not take them personally.

I had the opportunity to put this conversation into play, bringing "What was my part in it?" to an intrinsic conversation out of the darkness of knowledge and into the light of practice at a deep level. A while back I decided to do something different, namely to collaborate and build trainings with partners, two other people I trusted. They were creative, had influence, and were passionate about the same work I did: making a difference in the world. We formed a business together. We created a website, opened a bank account, created an operating agreement, and made verbal agreements on the disbursements of profits.

I was surprised at how smoothly and how fast things were going, and thought that maybe it would work. I was very comfortable with being a one-woman show. It was exhilarating, sharing ideas, collaborating, negotiating, and working through conflict.

As with most businesses, there were times when agreements needed renegotiating due to the evolution of lives, both personally and professionally. We continued to make those agreements and adjustments with each other, verbally, about the distribution of profits (and yes, there were profits). A percentage went to enrollment, and a percentage to training. Easy, right? Yes, until one partner overreached, and claimed and removed money she had not earned.

Some of you may be thinking that we should have had it all in writing, that no intelligent businessperson has verbal agreements. Slow down, partner, don't take that leap. There is some revealing, some unraveling that still needs to happen.

Seriously, this totally blindsided me. I felt broken nails and shards of glass in my gut and heart. I was distracted, felt disrespected, and my critical voice was louder than ever, pounding away in my mind about what a fool I was. As for the victim conversation … let's not even go there.

I started to pull gently at the thread, asking myself over and over: *What is my part? What is my part?* I had to move past the message: *You're a businesswoman, so you know you have to have signed agreements. No, not deep enough because, bottom line, a signed contract does not stop misconduct. Pull further. Start at the beginning.*

And yes, this took me about a week of intrinsic investigation. Then I found it. Yes, I thought, a visual so vivid, a bookmark in my memory.

When we were setting up our bank account and getting debit cards, I had the thought: *Should we all have equal access to the account? Isn't it just good business to have checks and balances, with two people's signatures needed to withdraw or release money?* I didn't bring it up because I didn't want them to think I didn't trust them.

Ugh, there it was: I was busy seeking their approval.

Now I had found my part in the outcome: a place of ownership, my neutrality. I could move forward.

My learning: Have the difficult conversations up front. There is relevance in the idea of trust and verify. Trust and verify is a standard to live by, personally and professionally.

Now you may be wondering what the difference is between my being accountable and what my part was in it. I am accountable for choosing not to share my concerns, not for my partner's actions. Accountability means diminishing the story around being a victim. To say I have a part in my results is turning reaction into response so I can find neutrality before I take action. Speaking and acting from a neutral position increases my desired outcome.

Part of being neutral is in knowing that reaction is normal. Reaction is going to happen, period. The key is in being aware of when we are in the state of reaction, and learning to interrupt ourselves and intervene before we take action. When we make choices from a responsive state, the outcome is more often aligned with our best interests, and the best interests of others.

This section is about grappling with concepts. Grappling in such a way that you will move from knowing the path, through continuing to have an intellectual conversation with yourself regarding these concepts, to walking the path. Own the conversations around the concepts and then put the concepts into action for the purpose of creating transformation. Keep working, practicing, and owning your neutrality.

Practice Page

In what ways do I create stress for myself?

In what ways do I create neutrality for myself?

In what ways do I create happiness for myself?

What is the payoff for turning reaction into response? What is the benefit from doing it differently?

Bring to mind a time when you felt, believed, thought that you had no part in the outcome. But the outcome affected you. Begin practicing the process of pulling the thread. Do this repeatedly until it becomes second nature.

Journaling Page

**Believe in the Power of You

Critical Voice

(Negative Self-talk)

Our critical voice is not our enemy. It doesn't need to be cut out and destroyed. We've simply given our critical voice way too much volume. It's time to turn down the volume and minimize the influence it has on our self-worth.

Jack Canfield, author of *Chicken Soup for the Soul*, states that 77 percent of our self-talk is negative. I believe there are days when it is higher than that.

Our critical voice records, stores, harbors, underlines, and bookmarks every mistake and failure we make, big or small. At the most inopportune moments it brings up the shame we feel in making these mistakes and failures. The shame arrives in full, living color, frame by frame, reciting the bright, yellow-highlighted, bookmarked passages word for word, all in the name of driving us to do better. It reminds us, for our own good, not to repeat our mistake, our failure. This mistake is attached to shame, and shame is not desirable.

The misconception is that the shame comes from the mistake. In reality the shame does not come from the mistake, but from the thought that we should have known better, we should have seen it coming, we should be perfect.

When we don't listen to the prompting of the critical voice, it gets louder and louder. The critical voice, driving us to do better, can appear as an overseer atop a cold, black stallion, bloodstained whip in hand, with bits of flesh hanging from the darkened strands, attempting to whip us into submission, bending us to its will. Or it may be the razor-sharp reprimands of an authority figure that berates and belittles us in the name of love.

With our permission, our critical voice has attached itself firmly to the conversation of doing better. We must be a better spouse, friend, mom, dad, sister, brother, aunt, uncle, child, neighbor, employee, supervisor, leader, member of the community, strategist ... the list goes on and on. This drive to do better is really a mask, and under the mask is the true agenda—to be perfect.

During a seminar I attended we were having a conversation around the pitfalls of perfectionism. An attendee raised his hand and the facilitator called on him.

"Wait," the attendee said, firmly and clearly. "The Bible states, 'Be ye therefore perfect.' So isn't that something we should be working towards?"

There was a tangible energy in the room, with mind whisperings that could almost be heard: *Are we going to talk about religion? Why would someone even bring up a Bible quote?*

The facilitator paused for a brief moment and responded in a way I will never forget. "It's true that Mathew 5:48 states, 'Be ye therefore perfect, even as your Father which in heaven is perfect,'" he said.

Most of us were stunned that he knew the exact verse.

"What if the word to focus on was *be*?" the facilitator continued, meaning to be in the moment. "Make your choices from the moment, not from the past or the future. Judge your path, and the people on the path with you in the here and now. If we're willing to live in the here and now, every choice we make will be perfect for us. In that moment we only have the information we have; we have what's in our hearts and our minds, and that's the perfect place to choose our next move from."

The room was pure silence as each of us grappled with the profound words of the facilitator. What if we took action in the moment, without all of our shame? What if we made choices free of worry about the future? What if we were more committed to being excellent than looking perfect?

There is a minimal but significant difference between living life in excellence and seeking and expecting perfection. The differences between perfection and excellence:

Perfection	Excellence
Right/wrong	Choices
No mistakes	Mistakes are seen as a learning opportunity
Fear	Excitement
Stagnant	Learning
Judgment	Accepting
Comfort zone	Risks
I am my results	Results

Success is a destination Success is a journey
Automatic/react   Conscious/respond
Image/ego   Authentic

Perfectionists are hard to be around because they hold us to the same standard of perfection that they hold themselves. This desire for perfection is a barrier between us. A barrier surrounded by razor blades, shards of glass, and barbed wire; a barrier that minimizes connection and maximizes shame. By being more committed to being excellent than appearing to be perfect, the critical voice has permission to be less demanding and loud.

The critical voice is not our enemy. The critical voice is operating in the past. We allow our critical voice to be the judge, jury and executor for our choices and decisions in the moment. Those choices range from those we choose to be in a relationship with (oh, they look like so-and-so; I remember how that person betrayed me in the past) to the ways we manage money (there's not enough/I make bad decisions about money) and everything in between.

Our critical voice has a specific role: to remind us to take notice of and learn from our mistakes, and to judge physical danger. Physical danger means taking notice if the burner is hot, the razor is sharp, there is black ice on the road, we need to wear sunscreen and stay hydrated.

When we don't heed the warnings or learn from our mistakes, shame creeps in. When shame is highlighted, we then hear: *That was stupid, how many times until you learn, idiot? I warned you that would make you fat ... and on and on and on.* We've become familiar with these thoughts and have begun to make them our truth.

When the critical voice berates us, we turn to the cheerleader voice to lessen the shame. The cheerleader voice can be just as problematic as the critical voice. The cheerleader is overly optimistic. This optimism promotes a form of denial. The cheerleader is trying to make us feel better about ourselves, and smooth over the shame inflicted by the critical voice.

The cheerleader voice: *No, you're not stupid; you're just fine, really. I know you're tired and don't want to get up and exercise, and that's OK. No, you're not a bad parent; you'll make it up to them.*

When shame and denial are the voices running us, we're playing an either-or game. By playing the either-or game, the critical voice and the cheerleader are two separate drivers creating a lack of mentality. When shame and denial are the voices running us, there is lack of forward movement, a lack of asking ourselves what's next, and definitely a lack of living in the moment.

What if it was not an either-or game? What if there was something truer than shame or denial? What if the forward movement—what's next, living in the moment—involved a new concept? A concept that put aside the shame and denial, and opened an internal conversation that included us being vulnerable. A conversation that was wholehearted.

By being willing to be vulnerable, you allow a wedge to be driven through shame and denial, a wedge that speaks to knowledge that there is something truer than the shame or denial. The wholehearted self is what is truer than the shame or denial

Brene Brown, PhD, LMSW, author and speaker, has brought credibility and scientific research to the connection of vulnerability and shame. She uses the word *wholeheartedness* in a significant way. In her book *Daring Greatly* she states, "Wholeheartedness, a way of engaging with the world from a place of worthiness."

I'm sure that many of you right now are running your critical voice: *There's no way I will be vulnerable. No way I will be taken advantage of, weak, open to being hurt.*

What if, in this conversation, this learning, you allowed yourself to look at vulnerability in a different light? What if being vulnerable meant the willingness to admit you made a mistake, knowing you are enough to handle the consequences? What if being vulnerable was asking for forgiveness from someone you wronged, knowing you're worthy of forgiveness whether they give it or not?

Through a willingness to be vulnerable, we bring wholeheartedness to our conversations and our lives. Approaching conversations and our lives in a wholehearted way means we bring *all* of us, all our flaws, failures, and mistakes, and all our successes, achievements, and qualities. We are all in; we are openhearted and wholehearted. We are worthy and enough.

As we begin to counter the critical voice and the cheerleader with the wholehearted voice, the volume of the first two is minimized. As we lean into a place of worthiness, we begin to inspire, enroll, and edify the self. Our self-talk no longer becomes an either-or conversation: either our critical voice or our cheerleader voice. Our self-talk begins to be conditioned to be in wholeheartedness automatically.

Wholeheartedness is a place that is familiar to us, but we have forgotten how to get there. It's a place as subtle as a spring breeze, carrying with it the sweet scent of promise. The promise that we are enough to handle what is placed in front of us. We are worthy of life's richest blessings. We have the sacred responsibility to care for ourselves in a wholehearted manner. We matter.

Our wholehearted self knows there's something truer than *I'm stupid, I'm fat, I'm a bad mother, father, spouse* and so on.

What is truer than I am a bad mom/dad?

- Critical self-talk: I am a bad mom/dad.
- Wholeheartedness/what is truer than: *I am the best mom/dad I know how to be.* (This statement gives room for choice, change, and action.)

What is truer than I am fat?

- Critical self-talk: *I am fat.*
- Wholeheartedness/what is truer than: *My body is a gift to be honored.* (This statement gives room for choice, change, and action.)

What is truer than I am stupid?

- Critical self-talk: *I am stupid.*
- Wholeheartedness/what is truer than: *I know what I know, and I'm learning every day.* (This statement gives room for choice, change, and action.)

When I share this technique during seminars, I often hear heart-wrenching evidence of the critical voice being made into truths. One young woman was struggling with her wholeheartedness, her *what is truer than,* and asked for coaching. I found her request very courageous, for there were over a hundred people in attendance, a handful of them her coworkers.

With tears about to spill over, and pain on her face, she said, "I am a mistake."

The room went deathly silent. I looked deep into her beautiful brown eyes, knowing she needed connection and wisdom, not my pity. "You have two statements you can choose from," I told her. "Either I matter, or I am a child of a loving God."

Her tears spilled over but a grin covered her face. "I'll take both," she proclaimed proudly.

Everyone let out the collective breath they had been holding and gave her a resounding round of applause.

We have given our critical voice way too much power for way too long. The critical voice is absolute and grounded in lack: *always, never, would have, could have, should have, if only, scarcity.*

Enough is enough. Today we take action to begin the process of lowering the volume, knowing that excellence is the goal and not perfection. We must live our lives in a wholehearted place of worthiness, a place of *what is truer than.*

Practice Page

Bring to mind one to three of your most common critical self-talks. Do not censor yourself. Write those thoughts under the Critical Self-talk heading. Bring to mind *what is truer than* those critical thoughts. Remember not to write double negatives. The critical voice has been too loud for too long.

Write the *truer than* thoughts under the Wholeheartedness heading. If need be, go back into the section and review the *truer than* examples.

Use this practice page over and over until you can do the *truer than* automatically in your thoughts. By using this page over and over, you will have visible evidence as to how far you've come in minimizing your critical voice.

Critical Self-talk	Wholeheartedness

Journaling Page

Trying on a New Thought

Values and Boundaries

Boundaries follow values. When we set boundaries based on our values, we create trusting relationships with self and others. Our values are our guiding principles, principles that are driven deeply into the ground that anchors our foundation.

Most societies have a structure based on values and boundaries. (When I reference "societies," I'm including all nations, religions, states, countries, political affiliations, clubs, groups, families, individuals, and so on.) In this chapter we will focus on individual values and boundaries.

Once you're clear on how you define your personal boundaries and values, you'll begin to notice how you're in alignment or out of alignment with other societies. By defining your values and boundaries, you can make large and small choices that will support you in living the life you design rather than a life that is lived by default.

As a facilitator of leadership seminars, I inevitably talk about time management. Most of us have many pressures, both personally and professionally, that need our attention from early dawn until hours after dusk. The key to time management is setting boundaries and learning to prioritize.

I also talk about prioritizing techniques, and how to handle interruptions, meetings and emails. These prioritizing techniques are based on time-management boundaries.

One day at a seminar a woman approached me with powerful feedback. She said that we toss out the word "boundaries," thinking most people know what the word means and how to set them. In my naive manner I think everyone knows what I'm talking about when I speak about boundaries.

By knowing our individual boundaries and values, we begin to live and share these with others, creating transparent, trusting, deep, and authentic relationships. Relationships where others know what they can count on from us, both personally and professionally: relationships that are in alignment.

Given that boundaries follow values, it's important that we identify our values and then build our boundaries on a value-based foundation. Our values are our guiding principles. Our values are driven deep into the ground to hold our foundations. Our values become the footings. Our values help to dictate our behavior and actions.

Most people have two or three main values. In order for your values to become footings in your life, each value demands a definition. This definition is how you, as an individual, define that value. One person's definition of a particular value may be totally different from another's. Values also need to include how the value shows up in behaviors/practices that are congruent with life choices.

By knowing and living our core values, we can have an influence on others. When we live by a set of core values, our lives takes on meaning and purpose. Challenging choices are easier to make. Failure is seen as opportunity. Success is woven with fulfillment. All of this becomes true when we're aligned with our guiding principles, our values.

Once you identify your own values, the next step is to define each one of those values. How do you define the word? Then, how does your value show up in behavior? Your definition and behavior in relation to a certain value may be entirely different to another person's.

My values are integrity, respect, and service:

- Definition of integrity: Living my authentic truth, walking the talk, doing the right thing even if no one is watching.
- How integrity shows up in behavior: Saying what I mean and meaning what I say; owning my mistakes and being accountable for my actions and results; focusing on what's next versus negativity and complaining.
- Definition of respect: Seeing others as a gift, regardless of their achievements, abilities, or qualities.
- How respect shows up in behavior: Being an attentive, authentic listener; honoring my agreements (including consequences); edifying, assuming positive intention.
- Definition of service: Being willing to give of my time and energy so others flourish and grow.
- How service shows up in behavior: Donating my time and money to those that want their lives to be different, and also knowing it's OK to charge for that time; knowing when self-care is needed and being OK with being selfish; giving permission to others to reinvent themselves and the world.

- People often ask me if personal values can change. Personally, I don't think so, but I can't say with factual sureness. After completing the worksheet, you will answer this question for yourself.

Around ten years ago I participated in a process of clarifying my values similar to the one included in this book. Integrity, respect, and service became clear to me at that time. As I looked back on my life I realized that these three values had always been guiding principles; I simply hadn't taken the time to identify, define, and recognize how they showed up in my behavior.

At this point in this section, you have a choice. You can go to the end of the section and use the worksheets provided to find your values, or you can continue reading about boundaries. I recommend you find your values before continuing, but again, it is your choice.

Boundaries are rules and agreements that are movable and negotiable. Making them movable and negotiable is based on the level of trust that has been earned, and the situation. Boundaries are put into place to provide structure for the "society." A simple example is children's bedtimes. When you're a child, your bedtime is significantly different from when you are a teenager, and then a college student, and then an adult.

There is an art to setting boundaries. We set boundaries for our well being and self-care. When we're willing to say no to others, we're saying yes to ourselves. When we're willing to be assertive with our boundaries, we're creating clarity for others.

The word *assertive* means to be direct and non-threatening; some of us are direct but threatening, and some of us are non-threatening but not direct. Assertive means to be both direct and non-threatening. The foundation of assertive communication is to create a win-win situation.

The following is an example of setting boundaries around material possessions. Do you loan your car to others? To whom, and what are the boundaries you set for the loan of your car?

You would probably assume that the vehicle would be returned in the same condition, the gas tank would be at the same level as it was when it was borrowed, all garbage and items would be removed, and there would be no damage. Do you state your conditions right from the beginning so the borrower can fulfill your expectations, or are you unclear and just make assumptions?

An expectation is a strong belief that something will happen in the future. An assumption is something we make up. You tell yourself that of course the borrower will return the car clean, with gas at the same level, and the vehicle undamaged. That is my level of commitment, so it most certainly will be theirs.

When you're unclear about your boundaries, and the car is returned on empty with garbage in it or damaged, you feel disappointed, disrespected, frustrated, and angry. But those feelings are on you because you were not clear about your boundaries. If you had clearly stated your boundaries, the borrower could have chosen to either borrow the car or not.

To continue with this example, you must also be clear about the consequences to the borrower of not returning the car in its original condition. Consequences are the byproduct of a lack of respecting others' boundaries. It's imperative that when you set a consequence for broken boundaries, you follow through. When you follow through, it creates consistency, and consistency creates respect.

Some of my children are on my phone plan. By being grouped together, we receive a discount. The boundary of being on the plan together is that they pay their portion by the fifth of each month. One of my children continued to break this agreement. I told him the next time he failed to pay his portion by the set date I would shut off his phone. It was not because I didn't have the money to float his share, I did. It was about setting boundaries based on values. He was out of alignment with my value of respect.

Sure enough, the next month rolled around and there was no payment. I contacted the phone company and shut off his phone. He has paid on time ever since. Me being willing to challenge our relationship and live my value has taken our relationship to a higher level of alignment.

In our personal and professional lives we have a limited number of resources: time, energy, money, and emotional and physical capacity. Many times we betray ourselves by not setting boundaries with others. We betray ourselves by putting others' needs and feelings first. We betray ourselves by believing we don't have rights, or we don't want to jeopardize a relationship. We betray ourselves by not being willing to say no if it means that others feel badly.

The person I find difficult to deal with is the person that says yes but really means no. In the end I pay for their inability to say no. I pay when they become passive-aggressive in their behavior and words. I pay when they don't fulfill their commitment and I'm scrambling to handle the dropped ball. I would prefer that they stated their truth and said no, rather than deal with the cost of them saying yes when they really meant no.

When we decide that we're as important as everyone else and set boundaries, we give permission for others to do the same. Being willing to say no takes courage and the willingness to let go of guilt.

Guilt is a productive emotion when we understand what the purpose of guilt is. Guilt is our signal that our beliefs and actions are out of alignment. In order to not feel guilty, we must change either our belief or our action. The problem comes when we don't do this, and simply talk ourselves back into alignment. When we talk ourselves back into alignment, the guilt will be repeated over and over.

Let's say that for the last two years you've been the chairperson of a cause you believe in. You're ready to step down at the end of your term. You've informed the president of the organization that you'll be resigning in a few months, at the end of your term. The president gently prods you to change your mind, claiming it will be hard to find someone as organized and dedicated as you, and you're beginning to feel guilty.

These feelings of guilt are attached to a belief of some kind. Your belief may be that you want to be seen to be contributing, but now you're quitting. This is when you might begin to justify, and try to talk yourself into realigning the belief and the action. Your justifying self-talk may look like this: *I've helped for two years; now it's someone else's turn.*

Your self-talk will probably only deepen the guilt, and then you relinquish your *no*: "Maybe they're right. What will it hurt to stay on for another two years?" You relinquish your *no* to stop the guilt, but nothing has changed, so then you feel resentment towards the circumstance and/or the other person. The cycle repeats again and again.

A powerful way of saying no assertively, and keep your beliefs and actions in alignment, is to satisfy the needs of both parties. You let the president know that you will not be serving a second term. You state that what you're willing to do is be available for two months to help the new chairperson. Your belief of contributing is satisfied and so are your actions.

It's OK to send our food back when it hasn't been prepared the way we asked for it.

It's OK to tell others: "I feel disrespected when I'm interrupted. Let me finish and then I'll be happy to listen to what you have to say."

It's OK to say no, and it also needs to be OK for others to say no to us. Being aware of our limits, and being willing to believe it's OK to self-care is necessary in setting clearly defined boundaries.

By knowing our values it's easy to set boundaries around what truly matters to us. We have the day-to-day opportunity to make it known to others where we stand. By knowing our values and setting clearly defined boundaries, we develop fulfilling relationships. When we know and live our boundaries and values, the consistency and alignment means that others trust the relationship. By being willing to set boundaries and live our values, we create a multitude of benefits for those around us and ourselves.

At the end of this chapter there is a worksheet to assist you in setting your boundaries.

Practice Page

Values Worksheets

This worksheet will take you through the discovery process and help you to identify your desires, which will lead to the unfolding of your values. Try not to judge your desires; there is no right or wrong desire. The more truthful you are in identifying your desires, the easier it will be to identify your values.

Have fun with this process of defining your values. By identifying your guiding principles, setting boundaries will become simplified.

Read through the List of Desires. In the column marked My Top Five, place a checkmark next to your top five desires. Then rank your marked desires from 1–5, with 1 being your top desire. Again, try not to judge yourself; there is no right or wrong, good or bad. Simply tell the truth.

List of Desires

Desires	My top five	In order 1–5
All the people in my life keep their agreements		
Others honor and listen to me at all times		
Spend a year in the Peace Corps on a Third World project		
People act on results, giving me no stories or excuses		
Become a member of the Fortune 500		
Excellent health throughout my entire life		
Always be clear about my direction and decisions		
World peace		
Master's degree(s) in a field(s) of my choosing		
Spend a year learning at the feet of the Dalai Lama		
Never experience loneliness		
Hold a public office of my choosing		
Have the perfect soul mate		
Live my life open and vulnerable		
See the world as a journey of happiness		
Speak my truth without repercussions		
Come and go as I please, and do whatever I like		
Be protected from physical injury throughout my life		
Have the capacity to let go of painful feelings		
Change one event in my life or in the life of another		
Be the richest person in the world		
Have no fear of the disapproval of others		
Be granted three wishes for whatever I want		
Always be right in any situation		
Have a one-time look into my future		

Next look over the List of Possible Values. Which words from this list can you associate with your top five desires? Example: *All the people in my life keep their agreements* could have an association with *trust*. Other words that could be associated with this desire are *accountability*, *respect*, *integrity*, and *freedom*.

The word you associate with the desire is the key. Circle the words you identify.

List of Possible Values

Commitment	Diversity	Accountability
Partnership	Acknowledgement	Vulnerability
Integrity	Respect	Service
Success	Health	Trust
Peace	Education	Spirituality
Connection	Influence	Love
Authenticity	Joy	Honesty
Freedom	Safety	Forgiveness
Compassion	Power	Wealth
Justice	Recognition	Risk
Fame	Unity	Wisdom
Possibilities	Career	Happiness
Acceptance	Adventure	Leadership
Humility	Intuition	Solitude

Now transfer the circled words into the Values table. Your final step will be to define the value and describe how that value shows up in your behavior/practices. This last part may take some time. Don't rush it. Examples have been given in the Boundaries and Values section.

One person's definition of a value and how it shows up in behavior/ practices can be very different from another's.

Values

Value	Value definitions	Behavior/practices

Setting Clearly Defined Boundaries

Below are some suggestions to be used as primers on your journey of setting boundaries.

- *Time:* When is your most productive time of day? When someone complains, suggest they offer a solution to their problem. Learn how to prioritize (see Steven Covey's Time Management Matrix). Notice when and why you procrastinate (see Eat that Frog! by Brian Tracey). What are you hoarding and why? (Hoarding includes not just physical items; we also hoard files on our computers). Keep a minute-by-minute journal for one week. (I know this will take time, but it's worth knowing who, what, and where you're spending your time.)

  Pay attention to where you need to set or adjust your boundaries.

- *Physical:* What is your level of comfortable social space? Do you give hugs or handshakes? In what way do you discern who gets which? What is your comfort level of eye contact? Where do you draw the line with nudity or state of undress? What words are permitted in your space? What kind of music do you want played around you? What is your limit of electronic interference when you're engaged in a conversation? What time of night do you prefer electronics to be shut down around you?

  Pay attention to where you need to set or adjust your boundaries.

- *Money:* To whom do you lend money? What conditions are in play for repayment? Are you willing to set up payments or do you want it back all at once? Do you charge interest? Do they have the ability to pay you back? Do you loan only if there's an asset you can leverage, or do you trust them at their word? Do you budget? Do you have discretionary income? If so, what do you spend it on? Do you follow your budget or cheat on it? Do you have a retirement plan? Is your money diversified? Do you see yourself as the steward of your money?

Pay attention to where you need to set or adjust your boundaries.

- *Energy level:* Where do you spend the majority of your energy? With whom do you spend the majority of your energy? Do you self-care, and if so how? Do you know and acknowledge when your energy levels are depleted and then say no? How often in a year are you sick? Are you willing to trade money for time; e.g. hire a housekeeper or gardener?
- Pay attention to where you need to set or adjust your boundaries.

These are just a few examples. Continue to list areas of your life around which you would like clear boundaries. Notice how I asked questions to probe the process of what, when, how, where, who, and why. I recommend setting boundaries in specific categories.

Most of us could use clearer boundaries in the area of relationships. Separate your relationships into sub-categories; e.g. social, volunteer, family (extended, immediate, in-laws) friends, and organized religion.

Remember, the purpose of setting boundaries is well being, self-care, and trust. By setting boundaries you create trust and alignment inside the "societies" of which you chose to be a part.

Journaling Page

**Words to Live By

Forgiving Self

Many of us are unwilling to forgive ourselves for fear we'll forget. Forgiving ourselves is about holding ourselves in a space of kindness, compassion, and love. Don't we deserve that?

Many of us have been preached to all our lives about the virtue of forgiving others. We hear about forgiving our neighbor from the pulpit of a multitude of religious denominations. We are quoted scriptures from religious and spiritual books about who is in charge of vengeance.

What if we focused just as much attention on forgiving ourselves as we do on forgiving others? What if we were as kind, compassionate, and loving to ourselves as we are to others? Many of you may be thinking, *Oh no, I can't do that. What I did was far worse. What I did was unforgivable.*

The reason it becomes unforgivable is because we continue to focus on *would have, should have, could have.* For some reason, we, as humans, love to live in the past or the future. We spend a large amount of our lives regretting our past or worrying about our future. The past cannot be changed, and the only way to predict the future is to create it in the present.

Beginning the process of forgiving self is acknowledging that the action began with a positive intention. That does not mean the outcome was positive; it simply means the action began with a positive intention.

My oldest daughter gave up a child for adoption. This was a conscious choice on her part. She researched and interviewed numerous applicants to parent, love, and raise her unborn child. For months my daughter and I had meaningful conversations about the emotional, physical, spiritual, and financial implications of her choice.

This choice of hers was out of my worldview and left me with a sense of trepidation. I even went into enabling and told her that I would raise her child until she was ready. She looked me straight in the eye and stated, "What kind of daughter and mother would that make me?" She was very clear about her decision. My job was to trust her and support her, and not get in her way.

When it was time to give birth, my daughter requested the adoptive parents not be present. She reassured them that she was committed to them being the parents of her child; she simply desired privacy in the birthing.

By law, the birth mother has a certain amount of time to change her mind before turning the baby over to the adoptive parents. When the nurse took the baby away for her checkup, my daughter requested that her daughter be returned to her rather than being kept in the nursery while the clock was ticking.

When it was time to deliver the baby to her family, I asked my daughter, for the last time, if she was sure about this.

"A good mother does what's in the best interest of her child," she said. "The family I've chosen is in the best interest of my child, period. Mama, this is also in my best interest."

As I watched my daughter walk down the hospital hallway carrying the child that came through her but not to her, I was filled with pride for her courage.

It was an open adoption. My daughter has had the opportunity to see her beautiful daughter turn into a thriving young woman. This young girl of fifteen has begun reaching out to my daughter. She has been raised knowing that she was adopted, and she has a desire and curiosity to meet her birth mother.

This reaching out has stirred the would-have, should-have, could-have conversations in my daughter, the internal stirring that sounds like: *What kind of mother gives away her daughter? I should have listened to others; I do feel regret. Maybe I could have done this. The most joyful day of their life was the most painful of mine. What I did was unforgivable.*

Forgiveness of our past choices is not always easy. Some of our choices, even from a place of positive intent, are hard to forgive. The reason these choices are hard to forgive is that we are looking at the event in the present moment.

It's imperative that we don't compare where we are today with when the event occurred. It borders on insanity to do so. In the present moment we are different. In the present moment we have new life choices, new life information.

Today, fifteen years later, my daughter would not make the same choice. However, fifteen years ago she made the best choice she could with the life lessons she had, in that moment. She is being mindful as she moves forward with the relationship while having the same positive intention: to do what is in the best interest of her daughter and herself.

When we're willing to remember that we're doing the best we know how, in the moment, we embrace imperfection. When we embrace imperfection, it's an easy leap to embrace forgiveness of self. Most of us don't think it's reasonable to hold others to a standard of doing everything right in every moment, so why do we hold ourselves to that standard?

Martha Beck, author and column writer, claimed: "Welcoming imperfection is the way to accomplish what perfectionism promises but never delivers." In other words, life is a journey of imperfections and lessons, not a destination to perfection. The promise lies in a life lived scarred, well worn, fulfilled.

We often think we must hang onto the event, the mistake, the offence, lest we forget. What if the letting go or the regret solidified the lesson we want to remember versus continuing the cycle of beating ourselves up?

Regret is the feeling of sadness or disappointment over something that has happened or been done, especially a loss or a missed opportunity.

A dear friend of mine spent over ten years not forgiving herself for an action she took when she was twenty. She was the only girl on a hunting trip. She had brought a tent to sleep in and the guys were sleeping in a camp trailer. The temperature had dropped dramatically throughout the day and she wasn't looking forward to the freezing night ahead. One of the men offered his jeep, with its warm heater, for her to sleep in. She jumped at the offer and took all of her gear and climbed into the warm jeep, mud-caked boots and all. She says she left mud everywhere in that jeep, and he probably had to clean mud off the ceiling.

She spent ten years regretting her actions. Regretting that she was not more careful. Regretting that she didn't notice, at the time, the mess someone else had to clean up. Regretting the actions of a "stupid twenty-year-old" (her words).

When we harbor regret, we're living in the past. Not forgiving our past can take a toll on our emotional and physical well being in the present.

After ten years, my friend made a phone call to the man who had generously allowed her to spend the night in his jeep. She apologized for her lack of care for his property. As she "cleaned up" her relationship with another, she minimized her regret by letting go of her past action. By making a simple phone call, she was able to begin the process of forgiving herself.

Minimizing regret begins with acknowledging that the outcome was not what we desired and then taking steps to make it whole. What I mean by making it whole is bringing it full circle; closing the gap between what we intended and the negative outcome.

Some people believe that making it whole requires an apology. Let me just say that the person you apologize to may not accept your apology. The apology is for *your* sake. By apologizing you are expressing your regret for some action, perceived or otherwise. By apologizing, you're acknowledging that there was some action not taken.

The other person may think that what you did was and is unforgivable. Remember, they don't know your intention, you do. Even if you try and convince them your actions were honorable, they may not be in the place to let it go, but you are. They may have their own self-loathing and regret going on around what occurred.

This is not about them; this is about you. Their forgiveness is not mandatory for you to forgive yourself.

Some people realize that bringing it full circle requires them to change their actions in the future. Learning from mistakes, events or outcomes allows transformational growth. "Transformational" means a major change in the way we show up in the world, being mindful of our past experiences versus regretting them.

Some people use education to teach others what they've learned. Many of you reading this are an influence on young lives. Instead of saying, "Don't do that," have a conversation about being mindful. Be the teacher, the guide, the messenger of your learning, and then let them find their own path.

Take action in a way that you believe will minimize your regret. Remember, this is not about the other person accepting your apology, never making that same mistake again, or expecting others to listen to your wisdom. The regret is yours; the forgiveness of self is yours. You must forgive yourself before you can fix yourself.

When we don't forgive ourselves of past faults it can cultivate and encourage fear; fear of how exposed we felt when we made a mistake, or the wrong choice; fear of not being trusted or trustworthy; fear of repeating the act that caused the regret.

The acronym F.E.A.R. has many alternative meanings. One of my favorites, found in the *Science of Mind* magazine, is "forget everything and run." Another is "face everything and rise." The choice is yours.

When we forgive ourselves, we have chosen to face everything and rise. By rising, we place ourselves in the spotlight of our lives. When we're willing to forgive ourselves, we spotlight our ability to feel kindness, compassion, and love for self. Most of us are not comfortable with treating ourselves with kindness, compassion, and love. We're especially not familiar with loving ourselves enough to forgive ourselves.

Bottom line: it takes courage to love yourself enough to forgive yourself. It takes courage to break the bonds of regret, blame, and self-loathing; courage to target the specific areas you feel are unresolved; courage to remember that your mistakes are not who you are; courage to have faith in yourself; courage to live in the present, spending your energy on change and forward movement; courage to be mindful versus perfect; courage to learn from the past and let it go.

We often hear the words, "Let it go." These three words have a significant meaning when linked with the story of how to catch a monkey.

The way to catch a monkey is to drill out a small hole in a tree, small enough for the monkey to slide its hand in right up to the wrist. Peanuts are then placed in the drilled-out space. The monkey reaches into the hole and wraps its hand around the peanuts, making a fist. When it tries to pull out its fist, it's caught. It's unwilling to let go of the peanuts so it hangs on and hangs on, even to its detriment. It becomes a prisoner to the payoff of peanuts.

The monkey hangs onto the belief of scarcity. It hangs onto the belief that these peanuts are all it has, regardless of the banquet of abundance in the world. All it has to do is let go of the peanuts—the payoff, the belief—and it will be free.

Everything we do, we do for a payoff. *Everything*—or we would not be doing it. Even negative attention is attention. When we're unwilling to forgive ourselves, we have our fists wrapped around a belief—a belief about what is good or bad, right or wrong, acceptable or not acceptable—and it keeps us a prisoner of our past. When we're unwilling to forgive ourselves for being human and making mistakes, we also become prisoners of our past. By letting go of this non-working belief, we are able to be free.

Forgiving ourselves is essential. When we forgive ourselves, we manage our reactions and emotions. When we forgive ourselves, we notice the good in the world versus all of the wrongs and other things we cannot change. When we forgive ourselves, we take the energy it took to harbor resentment, anger, or even hatred and focus it on forward movement and what's next. When we forgive ourselves, we give ourselves permission to be the person we're meant to be.

Forgiving self begins with remembering what our positive intention was in that moment. My friend: staying warm. My daughter: doing what was in the best interest of her daughter and herself.

Forgiving self is about living in the present versus the past or the future. We only have the gift of right now; that is why we call it the "present." We cannot change the past, and worrying about the future is a waste of precious time.

Forgiving self includes letting go of regret and focusing on forward movement. What action can you take in this moment? For this is the only moment you have.

Forgiving self is about accepting our imperfections. We are human and we're meant to learn from our mistakes; it's called growth. Fail faster, learn quicker; and then, forgive yourself and move on.

Forgiving self requires us to let go of beliefs that don't support our higher self, beliefs around good/bad, right/wrong, or acceptable/not acceptable. Supporting a higher self that resonates with kindness, compassion, and love.

Forgiving self takes courage, and the ability to face everything and rise.

Love and care enough about yourself to forgive yourself, regardless. You matter; live fearlessly in the present.

Practice Page

What event or mistake do you need to forgive yourself for? Begin with just one. I recommend you start small. By starting small you become familiar with the practicing and don't become overwhelmed. This practicing is like learning an instrument. We build our confidence with each level of understanding. We would fail if we started with a piece by Beethoven.

- What is your biggest regret regarding the event or mistake? (Yes, your regret deserves a voice—a *voice*, not a reason to stay attached to how unforgivable you are.)

- What action do you need to take to let go of the regret? (Apologizing, learning from it, teaching others, letting go of the payoff, something else?)

- What are your would-have, should-have, could-have self-talk dialogues that are running your unwillingness to let go of the past? (We only run this story because we're in a new place, with new information.)

- What belief are you tight-fisted about, holding onto? (A belief around right/wrong, good/bad, or acceptable/not acceptable is usually our payoff for not forgiving ourselves.)

· What was your positive intention at the time of the event or mistake?

· The action I will take moving forward in forgiving self is:

· Repeat three times: *I forgive me, I forgive me, I forgive me.* (Use this mantra as a pattern breaker. When your habit of unwillingness to forgive yourself creeps in, say three times: "I forgive me." Repeat as many times as necessary every day.)

Some of you may require a coach or a counselor of some kind as you are learning to forgive yourself. Sometimes we avoid asking others for help. We don't want to be seen as weak, incompetent, broken, a burden, not enough. Give yourself permission to seek any and all resources available to you in the practice of forgiving self.

Be patient with yourself as you begin practicing forgiveness of self. This will be a new process for most of you.

Journaling Page

Be Peaceful with Letting Go

Learning + Action = Transformation

As you begin to embrace and implement the concepts in this book, your level of influence and self-confidence will increase dramatically. There will be a tangible difference in the way you present yourself to your family, coworkers, friends, and the world. Some of these people may be skeptical and not trust the difference, some may see it as a threat and move out of your life, and some will be drawn to you and embrace you as a beloved friend.

When we're willing to show up differently, to reinvent ourselves, we give permission for others to do the same. Ann Voskamp states, "Practice is the hardest part of learning, and training is the essence of transformation."

A defining moment in my life occurred in a brief interaction with a stranger. I was given the opportunity to facilitate a two-hour session on conflict management in California. The attendees were the support staff from a school district, including custodians, grounds crew, nutrition workers, and so on. There were over five hundred attendees and they were each given the opportunity to pick the sessions they wanted to attend; there were twelve sessions to choose from.

He arrived ten minutes late, carrying a large chip on his shoulder. The other attendees in the room held their breath, and the air became electric as he stomped the length of the room towards an empty chair. He pulled the chair away from the group and the metal legs screeched against the linoleum floor.

I waited patiently while he got settled. When I began again, his hand shot up in the air. I called on him.

"Why are we here?" he asked defiantly. "What's so important that we need to spend a day in these stupid classes on these stupid subjects? Nobody gives a damn what we think."

He continued like a runaway train. "I have no idea what that guy was even talking about with his lofty speech this morning." He was referring to another trainer who had given the keynote. "I asked the instructor in my last class these same questions and she had no idea. What do you have to say?"

The other attendees looked down and away with an air of embarrassment and shame, giving me the impression that this was a pattern of behavior that occurred often.

There was a piece of me, my ego, that wanted to fight, be right, manipulate, and make wrong. I felt it, razor sharp, for just an instant, building in my chest and desiring to burst free from the back of my eyes.

Instead of giving into my desire to react, I chose to respond from a space of compassion: a place of walking what I talk, of having a clear purpose, of being neutral, of responding after I react, and of trusting me.

I looked directly at him. It felt like we were the only two people in the room. I stated in a wholehearted manner, "I really don't know the answer to your questions. My guess is you're here because someone holds you as valuable."

There was an immediate softening in the air and in him.

At the break he approached me, standing up close and in my personal space. Looking deeply into my eyes, he declared, "I'm sure you would never acknowledge this, but I bet you could bend us all to your will if you wanted to."

It took me back for a moment, and then I chose to continue to be openhearted with this man. "Oh, I'll admit that I could do just that," I said. "But why would I? I'd much rather enroll you, inspire you, empower you, and invite you to see the amazing person you are."

Hafez declares: "An awake heart is like a sky that pours light." It takes courage to live your life on purpose and transform into the person you're destined to be. Return often to the concepts in this guide. Living your life on purpose is a constant journey, not a destination.

My heart to yours, dear friend.

Journaling Page

**Brilliant Ideas and Amazing Thoughts

About the Author

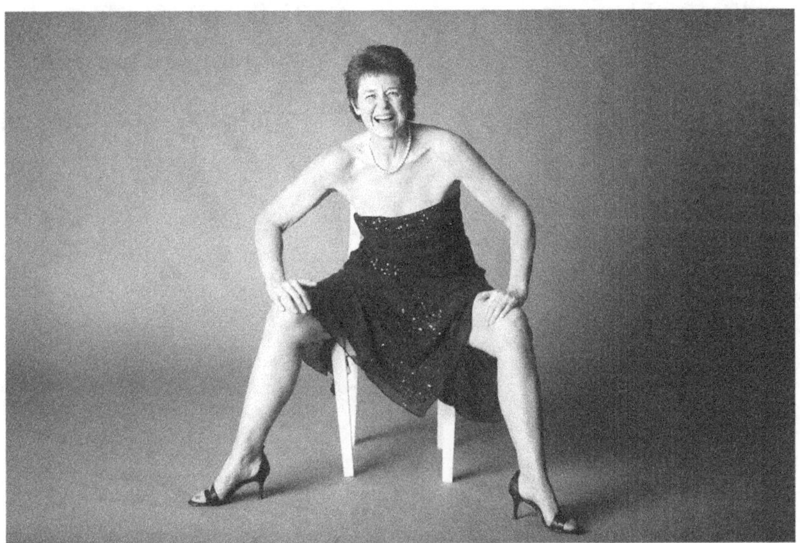

Kim Ashton is a transformational trainer, speaker, coach and author with fourteen years' experience in inspiring audiences, and guiding individuals to build powerful relationships and create intentional life results, both personally and professionally.

Kim travels the country, facilitating and mentoring leaders and executives. With focus on honoring individuality, Kim challenges audiences to open their minds to the idea of possibilities by letting go of ineffective paradigms and bearing witness to their own personal power.

With a unique ability to listen authentically, relate humorously, and inspire powerfully, Kim understands human-relationship dynamics. Her inquisitive and straightforward presentation style is complemented by an acute ability to get to the heart of the matter and make a profound impact. Kim is lauded for her ability to empower individuals with fundamental skills, tangible results, and the art of forward thinking.

Kim and her spouse reside in Provo, Utah, near Sundance Ski Resort. They are parents to six children and celebrate twenty-one grandchildren. She is founder of Kim Ashton International.